JAMES

PERCY

JUMP ON BOARD!

JOIN THE
THOMAS THE TANK ENGINE
FAN CLUB

*Bumper membership pack

*A birthday card from Thomas

*Further mailings

*Club newsletter 'The Thomas
Times' with each mailing

For more details about the Thomas Club either write to:-
Thomas The Tank Engine Club, Dept Buzz, PO Box 96,
Henley-on-Thames, Oxon RG9 2PQ or telephone 0491 411500.

First published in Great Britain 1993 by Buzz Books,
an imprint of Reed International Books Ltd
Michelin House, 81 Fulham Road, London SW3 6RB
and Auckland, Melbourne, Singapore and Toronto

ISBN 1 85591 293 7

Printed in Italy by Olivotto

Duck and Percy enjoy their work at the harbour, pulling and pushing trucks full of cargo to and from the quay.

But one morning, the engines were exhausted. The harbour was busier than ever. The Fat Controller promised that another engine would be found to help them.

"It's about time," said Percy.

"I ache so much I can hardly get my wheels to move," agreed Duck.

They waited for the engine to arrive.

It came as a shock when he did.

"Good morning," squirmed Diesel in his oily voice.

The two engines had not worked with Diesel for a long time.

"What are you doing here?" gasped Duck.

"Your worthy Fat er — Sir Topham Hatt sent me. I hope you are pleased to see me. I am to shunt some dreadfully tiresome trucks."

"Shunt where?" said Percy suspiciously.

"Where? Why from here to there ..."
purred Diesel "... and then again from there
to here. Easy, isn't it?"

With that, Diesel, as if to make himself
quite clear, bumped some trucks hard.

"Ooooooh!" screamed the trucks.

"Grrrrh," growled Diesel.

Percy and Duck were horrified. They did
not trust Diesel at all. They refused to work
and would not leave their shed.

The Fat Controller was enjoying his tea
and iced bun when the telephone rang.

"So, there's trouble in the harbour yard?
I'll be there right away!"

Diesel was working loudly and alone. Cargo lay on the quay. Ships and passengers were delayed. Everyone was complaining about the Fat Controller's railway. Percy and Duck were sulking in their shed.

"What's all this?" demanded the Fat Controller.

"Er, we're on strike, Sir," said Percy.

"Yes," added Duck. "Beg pardon, Sir, but we won't work with Diesel, Sir."

Then, in a quiet hurt voice, he added, "You said you sent him packing, Sir."

"I have to give Diesel a second chance. I am trying to help you by bringing Diesel here. Now you must help me. He was the only engine available."

Percy and Duck went sadly back to work.
Next morning, things were no better.
Diesel's driver had not put his brakes on
properly and Diesel started to move.

He went bump, straight into Percy!

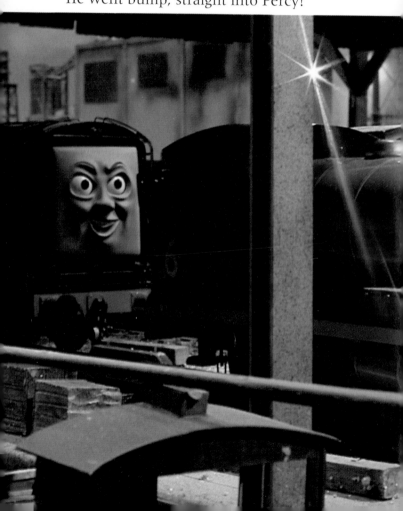

Percy had an awful fright.

"Wake up there, Percy," scowled Diesel.

"You have work to do."

He didn't even say he was sorry to Percy.

Later, Diesel bumped the trucks so hard that the loads went everywhere.

"What will the Fat Controller say?" gasped Percy.

"He won't like it," said Duck.

"So who's going to tell him, I wonder?" said Diesel. "Two little goody-goody tell-tales like you, I suppose."

Percy and Duck did not want to be tell-tales, so they said nothing.

Diesel, thinking he could get away with his bad behaviour, was ruder than ever.

Next day he was shunting trucks full of china clay. He banged the trucks hard into the buffers, but the buffers weren't secure.

The silly trucks were sunk.

Soon the Fat Controller heard the news. The trucks were hoisted safely from the sea, but the clay was lost.

The Fat Controller spoke severely to Diesel.
"Things worked much better here before you
arrived. I shall not be inviting you back."

"Now Duck and Percy, I hope you won't mind having to handle the work by yourselves again."

"Oh no, Sir. Yes please, Sir," replied the engines.

Whistling cheerfully, they puffed back to work while Diesel sulked slowly away.

THOMAS

EDWARD

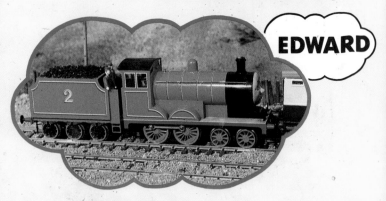

GORDON